Ruby's Baby Brother

For Ivy, Jasper and Seth. Three shining lights . . . — K. W.

To my new baby boy, Leon. You are such a delight. I love you squillions xx — M. L.

Barefoot Books
2067 Massachusetts Ave
Cambridge, MA 02140

Text copyright © 2013 by Kathryn White
Illustrations copyright © 2013 by Miriam Latimer
The moral rights of Kathryn White and Miriam Latimer have been asserted

First published in the United States of America by Barefoot Books, Inc in 2013
The paperback edition first published in 2013

Graphic design by Judy Linard, London, UK
Color separation by B & P International, Hong Kong
Printed in China on 100% acid-free paper
This book was typeset in Triplex and Hoagie Infant
The illustrations were prepared in acrylic paints and watercolor pencils

Hardback ISBN 978-1-84686-864-1
Paperback ISBN 978-1-84686-950-1

Library of Congress Cataloging-in-Publication Data
is available under LCCN 2012020205

1 3 5 7 9 8 6 4 2

Ruby's Baby Brother

Written by **Kathryn White**

Illustrated by **Miriam Latimer**

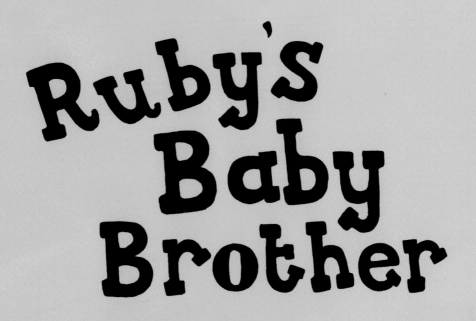

Barefoot Books

step inside a story

Mom's coming home with Leon today.
I'm **nervous** and wonder
if he's here to stay.

Babies are **smelly**;
they make too much **noise**.
And Leon is bound
to snatch all my toys.

So I've just made my wand
and a big starry hat,
and I think I'll turn Leon
into a **bat**.

Then I'll open the window,
and out he will fly,
and sleep upside down
in the oak tree nearby.

Suddenly Mom and Leon are here.
It's **Strange**, and it's **Scary**.
I dare not go near.

I secretly peek my head around the door.
I wonder if Mom is the same as before.

Is she holding a baby — or is it an elf?
He's bound to have **magical powers** himself.
What if he says to me, "This is **MY** house.
So, Ruby, I'm turning you into a **mouse**."

I'll live in this **mousehole** deep under the stairs,

and sneak out for **bread crumbs** from under the chairs.

Then Dad kneels beside me.
He says, "Come and see.
He looks just like you.
He's as **sweet** as can be."

I hear a strange **gurgle**
and **hiccupy** noise.
I don't want to see him.
I **hate** little boys!

This **isn't** my brother!
He's come from the stars.
He looks like a **creature**
from Pluto or Mars.

I'm making this rocket
up here in my room,
I'll blast **Martian** Leon
right up to the moon.

Now Leon is **wailing**;
trust him to cry.
Mom says he's **pooey**,
that's probably why.
Dad's going to change him
— a fun thing to do!

But what about me? **Look** – I'm here too!

Then Mom hugs me tight,
and we sit on a chair.
She's talking and laughing
and braiding my hair.

Dad gives me Leon
who opens his eyes.
He clutches my finger.
I **laugh** in surprise.

His hand is so tiny;
he's so **warm** and **small**.
I wrap myself all around him
in one cuddly ball.

I'm a **busy** big sister;
    there's so much to do.
I find all my paper,
    my crayons and glue.

These are our swords
   for the battles we'll fight
when we're riding on quests
   as a **queen** and a **knight**.

This hat that I've made
   he'll wear every day.
When he's a **captain**,
   we'll sail on the bay.

I'll battle fierce **serpents**
that rise from the sea,
and then rescue Leon
with this golden key.

And these are his wings.
When he's ready to **fly**,
we'll both build a castle
high up in the sky.

And I'll use my spells
and my magical power
to tame fiery **dragons**
that circle the tower.

This spaceship will help us
to **zoom** far away.
Leon will steer,
and I'll tell him the way.

Whizzing faster than light,
we'll shoot into space,
and wave at our house
from some far distant place.

But when it is night,
and the moon's shining high,
when **witches** and **wizards**
and **ghosts** start to fly,
when he's lying afraid
of a **creak** on the stair,
he won't have to worry:

I will be there.